Anne of Avonlea

Retold from the Lucy Maud Montgomery
original by Kathleen Olmstead

Illustrated by Dan Andreasen

STERLING CHILDREN'S BOOKS
New York

STERLING and the distinctive Sterling logo
are registered trademarks of Sterling Publishing Co., Inc.

Library of Congress Cataloging-in-Publication Data

Olmstead, Kathleen.
  Anne of Avonlea / retold from the Lucy Mead Montgomery original ; abridged by
Kathleen Olmstead ; illustrated by Dan Andreasen.
    p. cm. — (Classic starts)
  Summary: An abridged version of the tale of Anne, an eleven-year-old orphan,
who comes to live on a Prince Edward Island farm and proceeds to make an indelible
impression on everyone around her.
  ISBN-13: 978-1-4027-5424-1
  ISBN-10: 1-4027-5424-8
  [1. Orphans—Fiction. 2. Friendship—Fiction. 3. Islands—Fiction. 4. Country
life—Prince Edward Island—Fiction. 5. Prince Edward Island—History—20th
century—Fiction. 6. Canada—History—1867–1914—Fiction.] I. Andreasen, Dan, ill.
II. Montgomery, L. M. (Lucy Maud), 1874–1942. Anne of Green Gables. III. Title.
  PZ7.O499An 2009
  [Fic]—dc22

                                                                    2008001965

Lot#:
6 8 10 9 7 5
02/17

Published by Sterling Publishing Co., Inc.
387 Park Avenue South, New York, NY 10016
Text copyright © 2009 by Kathleen Olmstead
Illustrations copyright © 2009 by Dan Andreasen
Distributed in Canada by Sterling Publishing
$^{c}/_{o}$ Canadian Manda Group, 165 Dufferin Street,
Toronto, Ontario, Canada M6K 3H6
Distributed in the United Kingdom by GMC Distribution Services,
Castle Place, 166 High Street, Lewes, East Sussex, England BN7 1XU
Distributed in Australia by Capricorn Link (Australia) Pty. Ltd.
P.O. Box 704, Windsor, NSW 2756, Australia

Classic Starts is a trademark of Sterling Publishing Co., Inc.

Printed in China
All rights reserved

Sterling ISBN 978-1-4027-5424-1

For information about custom editions, special sales, premium and
corporate purchases, please contact Sterling Special Sales
Department at 800-805-5489 or specialsales@sterlingpublishing.com.

CONTENTS

CHAPTER 1

An Irate Neighbor

ᥨᦓ

It was a warm, sunny day in August. A light breeze was blowing, and there was not a cloud in the sky. A slim sixteen-year-old girl with serious gray eyes and long auburn hair was sitting on the front steps of a farmhouse on Prince Edward Island.

Anne Shirley was reading a book of poetry. She had been saving the book for a sunny day, but now that she was enjoying the lovely breeze and the poppies blowing in the yard, she lost all interest in it. This was a day better suited for dreams.

The heavy book of poetry fell to her feet as Anne's mind wandered to the new school year. She was about to start her new job as the teacher at Avonlea School.

She imagined a time in the future—forty years or so—when a former student would return for a visit. In her dream, Anne could not decide if this student would be a college president or a member of the Canadian Senate. She only knew that he would be very successful. He would return to Avonlea to thank his old teacher and tell her that he never would have been so successful if it weren't for her devotion and hard work.

Suddenly Anne's pleasant dream was disturbed by a Jersey cow trotting into the yard. Immediately following the cow was Mr. Harrison. He was their new next-door neighbor. Anne had never met him, although she had seen him a few times. Actually, very few people had met Mr.

Harrison, even after several months in Avonlea. Those who did know him called him a crank.

Mr. Harrison burst into the yard and stomped toward Anne. "What is the meaning of this?"

"Excuse me?" Anne said, standing up and placing her hands on her hips.

Anne had already heard stories about Mr. Harrison. Mrs. Lynde had visited his house and said it was a mess. He only washed his dishes on rainy days. He never swept the floor. He ate his meals at strange times. Then, to top it all off, he had a pet parrot. No one in Avonlea had ever had a pet parrot before!

"I'm sorry, Mr. Harrison," Anne said sharply. Unfortunately, Anne had quite a temper, and she thought he was very rude for bursting into her yard without even a hello. "I don't understand what you are talking about."

"That cow!" He pointed to the cow still standing in the front yard. "This is the third time I found your Jersey cow in my oats! Where is your aunt? I want to speak to her right away."

"If you mean Miss Marilla Cuthbert," Anne said sternly, "she is not my aunt. She and her brother, Matthew, were kind enough to take me in from an orphanage when I was young. And, no, Miss Cuthbert is not at home. She is visiting a sick relative."

"Then who will deal with this cow?" Mr. Harrison shouted. "She's eating all my oats!"

"I will deal with the cow," Anne said. "She belongs to me, not Miss Cuthbert. And I think this problem might be solved if you took better care of your fences."

"You have some nerve, young lady. My fences are fine, and no red-headed youngster will tell me otherwise."

"Red-headed!" Anne was furious now. "I have auburn hair, not red. And I'll have you know that I would rather have red hair than no hair at all!"

Mr. Harrison's face grew bright with anger.

"I am sorry to be rude," Anne said. "I should try to be considerate and imagine your side. It must be difficult to find a cow in your oats. Thankfully, a good imagination is one of my strengths. But it is difficult to have a good imagination when someone is so rude."

Mr. Harrison was about to speak, but Anne cut him off.

"Thank you for your visit, Mr. Harrison," she said. "I will make certain that Dolly is locked in our yard. I give you my word that you will not find her in your oats again."

After Mr. Harrison left, Anne locked Dolly in the milking pen. "You stay put now," she said, and checked the latch on the gate twice before heading back to the house.

When Marilla returned later that afternoon, Anne prepared tea for them both. She told Marilla about Dolly and the oats.

"That cow can be a nuisance," Marilla said with a sigh. "I'll be glad when the auction is over. We need to sell all our livestock. It's been too hard since Matthew died."

Anne took a deep breath. She still had to fight back tears when she thought of him. Anne had vowed to wear black every day as a tribute to dear, sweet Matthew.

"How was your cousin Mary?" she asked to take her mind off Matthew.

"She's actually my third cousin, but I suppose family is family." Marilla was a very practical person. "She is not doing well. Her doctor says she might not last the month. I'm very worried about her twins. They're only six years old."

"My goodness," Anne said. "What will happen to them?"

"Mary has a brother in British Columbia, but he can't take them right now. He is working as a logger and won't return from the woods until spring."

"Oh, Marilla. I hope it will work out. I know how hard it is to be alone in this world. I was all alone until you and Matthew took me in."

"We'll just have to wait and see," Marilla said. Once again, she was being very practical. There was no sense worrying about something before it happened.

"Now, Anne," Marilla continued. "Is there any news since I've been away?"

"Oh, yes, Marilla! An awful lot has happened in the past three days," Anne said, glad to change from a topic as sad as orphan twins. She told Marilla all about the Avonlea Village Improvement Society. She, her dearest friend Diana Barry, Gilbert Blythe, and a few others were starting it.

"We want to improve the look of Avonlea,"

Anne explained. "We'll paint the Community Hall, fix fences around town, and ask Mr. Boulter to tear down the old shack on his property. It is an awful-looking old thing. I'm amazed it still stands on its own!"

"Oh, Anne," Marilla said. She almost broke into laughter. "Levi Boulter will not tear down his shack. He's a stubborn old goat of a man."

"Well, we're certainly going to try," Anne said. "I can be very determined, you know."

This time, Marilla did laugh. She also shook her head. "Yes, Anne. I am well aware how determined you can be."

CHAPTER 2

Dolly Escapes Again

A few days later, Anne and Diana Barry decided to go shopping. As they rode home in their carriage, they discussed the Avonlea Village Improvement Society and the old house on Mr. Boulter's land.

"Marilla said that another family used to live there," Anne said. "She said it used to be quite lovely. The family had many children, and the house was full of laughter. Mr. Boulter bought the land when they moved. He built a new house but never bothered tearing the old one down.

Now there is only the wind whipping through it. I find deserted houses so sad. I imagine all kinds of stories about the family. I wonder what happened to them and why they left. Once my mind starts spinning, there is no stopping me."

"Not me!" Diana laughed. "I don't let my imagination get the best of me anymore. Once, I imagined the woods were haunted, and I was so terrified I couldn't go near them for weeks. That was enough for me, thank you."

Anne shook her head slightly. She loved Diana dearly, but it was not easy having a best friend with so little imagination.

"Oh, no!" Anne suddenly cried and stopped their carriage. She pointed to Mr. Harrison's farm. Standing in the middle of a field of oats was a Jersey cow.

Before Diana understood what was happening, Anne had jumped from the carriage and started across the field. Diana quickly followed.

The two girls struggled through the oats to the cow, their long skirts and laced-up boots quickly becoming covered in mud. Anne grabbed the rope around the cow's neck and slowly pulled her back to the carriage.

Just then Mr. Shearer, one of their neighbors, arrived. He and his son were heading toward Carmody. They stepped down from their carriage.

"Do you need any help, Anne?" Mr. Shearer called.

Anne was out of breath. It was hard work dragging a muddy skirt across a field, not to mention a cow!

"Dolly got loose again," she said, sighing heavily. "I have to get her before more damage is done."

"She's a good-looking cow," Mr. Shearer said. "Are you still interested in selling? We're on our way to Carmody to sell livestock, and I'm sure we

can find space for one more. I'll give you twenty dollars."

"Oh, Mr. Shearer." Anne smiled. She thought of hugging him but restrained herself. That was something young girls did—not girls of almost seventeen. "That would be wonderful. I have to admit that Dolly has been a lot of trouble."

So the deal was made. Mr. Shearer took Dolly to Carmody, and Anne and Diana continued on their way.

After she dropped off Diana, Anne returned to Green Gables, as her home was called. Marilla had just set out the tea.

Anne was cutting some bread by the sink, telling Marilla about all her purchases, when she happened to look out the window. She stopped talking—not an easy task for Anne—and froze.

Marilla looked up from her tea. "Anne," she called. "What is the matter?"

"D-d-d-dolly," Anne stammered.

"Dolly? Your cow?" Marilla was confused. "What about Dolly?"

"She's standing in the milking pen."

"Well, of course she is," Marilla said. "Where else would she be?"

"You don't understand, Marilla." Anne started to cry.

"You are right about that," Marilla said. "I don't understand at all."

"Marilla," Anne turned around to look at her. "If Dolly is in the milking pen, that means that I sold Mr. Harrison's cow instead!"

CHAPTER 3

Mr. Harrison at Home

ｃ∽

Anne was in quite a state. She had accidentally sold her neighbor's cow. Now what was she to do?

"Anne," Marilla said. "Please stop fretting. You'll have to go to Mr. Harrison's and explain what happened."

"I know I must confess," Anne whimpered. "It's only that Mr. Harrison is so cranky. Of course, he has every right to be furious with me. But I'm not anxious to experience it face-to-face."

Marilla patted Anne on the back. She handed the girl her hat and gently pushed her toward the door.

Anne walked slowly down the lane toward Mr. Harrison's farm. When she saw him sitting on the front porch, she stopped. She took a deep breath and opened his front gate.

As soon as Mr. Harrison saw Anne, he jumped up from his chair and ran into the house. The door slammed behind him.

Oh, my, Anne thought. *He is furious with me already.* She slowly made her way up the front steps. It took a great deal of courage to knock on his door.

Mr. Harrison answered. He smiled shyly at Anne and invited her in. He appeared quite nervous. Anne noticed that he had put on his coat and brushed his hair.

"I-I'm sorry about that," he said. "I wasn't expecting any visitors."

"I understand perfectly, Mr. Harrison," Anne said. "I didn't expect to stop by."

Mr. Harrison offered Anne a seat. Then, just as she was about to sit, Anne heard another voice.

"What's the red-headed girl doing here?" the strange voice said.

Both Anne and Mr. Harrison's faces turned red, but for different reasons. Anne turned around to find out who was being so rude and saw a parrot perched on a shelf.

"That's Ginger," Mr. Harrison said. "My brother, who was a sailor, gave him to me. He's rather rude, but I have to admit that I'm very fond of the old bird. He's the only company I've got."

"Silly red-headed girl," Ginger repeated.

"Try to ignore him, Miss Shirley," he said. "Now, how can I help you?"

"Well," Anne said. She sat up straight in her chair. "This isn't an easy thing to say, Mr.

Harrison. So, please, let me say it all without interruption."

Mr. Harrison nodded.

"As you know, Mr. Harrison, you have found my cow Dolly in your oats a few times."

"What? You don't mean that your cow is in the oats again?" Mr. Harrison leaned forward in his chair.

"No," Anne said. "Not the oats."

"Not the wheat!" he said. Mr. Harrison leaned so far forward that he was almost on his feet.

"No, Mr. Harrison," Anne replied. "Not the wheat. Now please, sit back and let me tell the story. And remember, no interruptions."

Mr. Harrison leaned back, but Anne noticed that he was still gripping the chair arms.

"My best friend, Diana Barry, and I were returning from a shopping trip in Carmody. This afternoon was quite lovely—I'm sure you remember—and we were enjoying our trip. That's when I noticed a Jersey cow in your oats."

Mr. Harrison was about to speak but remembered his promise. He remained quiet.

"So, knowing how upset you would be, Diana and I rescued the cow from the field. When we got back to the carriage, we met Mr. Shearer and his son. Now, Mr. Shearer was on his way to Carmody. He was selling some cattle and offered to buy Dolly for twenty dollars. Since she was causing so much trouble and Marilla was selling most of our stock anyway, I said yes."

"That seems wise," Mr. Harrison said. "But what does it have to do with me?"

"That's what I'm getting to, Mr. Harrison," she said. "When I returned to Green Gables, I discovered Dolly in the milking pen. So you see, this means only one thing. I sold your cow to Mr. Shearer!"

"That does seem to be the case," her neighbor replied. He sat quietly in his chair. Anne was surprised by his calm reaction.

"I'm really very sorry, Mr. Harrison. Unfortunately, your cow is long gone by now. I could give you the twenty dollars that Mr. Shearer gave me. Or, if you prefer, I could give you Dolly. She is a good cow. I've had her since she was a calf."

Mr. Harrison thought for a moment. "I think I'll take your cow. If she's as good as you say, of course."

"Yes, yes, she is," Anne said. "I may have a bad habit of having adventures, but I never lie."

"I guess that settles it, then," Mr. Harrison said. "Can I offer you a cup of tea, Miss Shirley? It rained yesterday, so all the dishes are clean. I just don't see the point of using the water pump when rainwater will take care of it."

"That would be wonderful," Anne said with a

smile. "But please, let me make it for you. You've been so kind, it's the least I can do."

"I'm sure you were frightened to death to come," Mr. Harrison said. "I suppose I should apologize, too. I put on quite a show the other day. I'm sorry that I yelled at you."

Anne laughed. "It would seem that we are quite the pair."

Anne made the tea and put out bread and butter. After a quick search through his cupboards, she also found a can of peaches. She and Mr. Harrison sat at the table and spent a very pleasant afternoon together.

When it was time for Anne to leave, Mr. Harrison walked her to his front gate.

"I hope that you won't be too much of a stranger, Miss Shirley," he said. "Now that you know I'm not so cranky, perhaps you will stop by once in a while. I would be very happy for the company."

"I promise that I will," Anne said. "Even if it does mean putting up with Ginger's rude comments." She laughed and waved as she walked down the lane.

When she returned home, Anne found Marilla preparing dinner in the kitchen.

"Isn't it a wonderful world?" Anne asked. "I made a very silly mistake, and I ended up making a new friend. Don't you think that is wonderful, Marilla?"

"Anne Shirley," Marilla replied, "I will always be surprised by the silly things you say."

Anne smiled at Marilla and started peeling potatoes.

CHAPTER 4

A New Life as a Teacher

〜

It was the night before the first day of school. Anne, Jane Andrews, and Gilbert Blythe were standing at the fence near Green Gables's front gate admiring the sunset.

"I think you are both very lucky," Anne said. "You will be teaching new children. Almost all of my students will be former classmates."

Anne was teaching at the Avonlea School where she, Jane, and Gilbert had all been students. Jane was going to the New Bridge School and Gilbert to White Sands.

Anne had planned to go to college, but her plans had changed. First the bank where Marilla kept all of her money went out of business, and she lost her savings. Then Marilla's brother, Matthew, died suddenly. Marilla simply could not afford to send Anne to school, and so Anne had decided to teach.

Gilbert had generously given up his teaching job at Avonlea. He would take a job in White Sands so Anne could stay close to home and help run the house. It was a wonderful solution for all of them.

"Mrs. Lynde says that they will never respect me as a teacher," Anne said.

"Anne," Gilbert said, chuckling, "you must realize by now that Mrs. Rachel Lynde only considers the bad side of things."

"Oh, I know," Anne said. There was a time when she never would have agreed with Gilbert.

They had been great rivals, but now they were friends, and Anne was very glad.

"However," Anne continued, "I think she does have a point this time. I don't want an unruly classroom."

"You will simply have to be firm," Jane said. "I intend to be very strict with my students. I will not tolerate any rude behavior." Jane was kind and had a good heart, but she did not like anything out of order.

"Oh, I have no intention of being so strict," Anne exclaimed. "Our old teacher, Miss Stacy, taught us with kindness. I want my students to *want* to learn. I don't want them studying because they are afraid of me. What do you think, Gilbert?"

This was a difficult question for Gilbert. He wanted to impress Anne, but he also wanted to speak his mind.

"Well," he said, "I think you need to judge each student differently. Some will respond to kindness. Others will need more."

"I think you are both wrong," Anne said. "Punishment does not help children learn."

"I suppose," Jane said slyly, "if a girl misbehaves, you could punish her by sitting her next to a boy."

Anne and Gilbert looked at each other and smiled shyly. Many years ago, Anne had been forced to sit beside Gilbert as punishment.

After her friends said good-bye, Anne walked slowly back to the house. As she walked, she thought about her life since coming to Avonlea.

It did not seem so long ago that she had first arrived at Green Gables. Yet she was no longer the same little orphan girl. She was excited to start her new life in the morning, but she was also sad. She must say good-bye to childhood.

Being a teacher was an adult job. Her world was changing.

༄

At breakfast the next morning, Marilla could tell that something was wrong. She asked Anne why she looked so concerned.

"Oh, Marilla," Anne said. "What if I fail? What if today is terrible and I am an awful teacher?"

"You'll not ruin everything in a single day," Marilla scoffed. She gave Anne a cup of ginger tea. "My, how you worry about silly things!"

Anne was so deep in her own thoughts that she barely heard Marilla. In fact, Anne barely noticed anything on her way to the schoolhouse. She did not stop once to smell the flowers or admire the trees. That was very unlike Anne.

At the school, she found a room full of

smiling and curious faces. Anne had stayed up late the night before preparing a speech. She had rehearsed it so many times that she knew it by heart. It was an inspiring speech about the power of learning and working together. Now, unfortunately, she could not remember a single word.

Instead, she said faintly, "Please take out your readers." Anne collapsed into her chair. She hoped her students did not notice her red face.

Anne knew most of the children, of course, but she did notice one new face. Sitting quietly by himself was a ten-year-old boy named Paul Irving.

Anne had already heard stories about Paul from Marilla and Mrs. Lynde. Paul's father, Stephen, had moved to the United States many years earlier. When his wife had died, Stephen had sent Paul back to Avonlea to live with his grandmother.

Anne immediately recognized a kindred spirit in Paul. He had a serious face but bright,

questioning eyes. She knew instantly that they would be friends.

Anne felt like she was in a dream the entire day. She finished all the lessons, but they were a blur to her. She did remember Andrew Pye pouring water on Aurelia Clay's neck, though. She kept him inside at recess and explained why it was wrong. Even though Andrew did not seem bothered by his punishment, Anne thought she had done the right thing.

When school was over, Anne sat alone in the classroom. She was disappointed by her first day. She worried that she might not like teaching. *Wouldn't it be terrible,* Anne thought, *if I spent forty years doing something I disliked?*

Anne walked home slowly, thinking all the way.

Her first day as a teacher was over. Nothing had gone wrong, but she wanted to make sure the next day was better.

CHAPTER 5

Anne and Gilbert Make Plans

✎

October on Prince Edward Island was one
of Anne's favorite times of the year. The weather
was still warm and leaves were starting to
turn their fall colors. Anne was always happy
to take long walks over the red dust roads
in this weather. Quite often, a soft wind over
the sand dunes brought with it the smell of
the sea.

On one such Saturday afternoon, she and
Diana were walking along the road. They were
going door-to-door to raise enough money for

the Avonlea Village Improvement Society to paint the Community Hall.

The two girls weren't having much luck, though. Most people were not interested. They bid the girls farewell before they could even finish their opening speech.

Mrs. Sloane was angry because she thought the Improvement Society wanted to rip up roadsides and plant flowers. This seemed rather pointless to her. Miss Eliza Andrews thought trying to improve the village was a waste of time. Mr. and Mrs. Fletcher refused even to answer the door, although Anne had seen them on the porch a moment earlier.

Some people used their visit as an excuse to complain about other people. Mr. Wright wanted the society to tell Mr. Sloane to keep his beard trimmed. Mr. Spencer said he would give money to the society if someone finally kept the church walk shoveled in the winter.

Anne decided to try one more house. She stopped by Mr. Harrison's to ask for his support and found him enjoying the sunset with Ginger at his side. Since the day of her confession, Anne had often visited Mr. Harrison. She felt certain that he would show his support with a small donation.

"I'm sorry, Anne," he said. "I think your society is a fine idea, but I'm not one for donating."

Anne sighed. "I'll be honest," she said. "If I have another day as discouraging as this one, I'll start to believe Miss Eliza Andrews is right!"

The next day, Anne was sitting at the kitchen table surrounded by papers. She was lost in thought and did not hear Gilbert at the open door.

"What's the matter?" he asked. "You look worried."

Anne smiled at Gilbert. She waved her hand to indicate that he should come inside. "I'm just reviewing my year so far," she said. "I just don't know if I'm succeeding. Am I reaching all of my students?"

"Anne," Gilbert said gently. "You're too hard on yourself. You're a wonderful teacher, and all your students adore you."

"Not all," Anne replied. "Anthony Pye still doesn't respect me. He doesn't misbehave any more than the others, but he often sneers at me. The trouble is, I know that he's a nice boy deep down."

"I think he's had a hard life," Gilbert said. "Maybe he'll come around."

"Maybe," Anne said. "At least there is one student I am very happy about—Paul Irving."

"He does seem like a nice young man," Gilbert agreed. He always enjoyed watching

Anne when she was excited. Her gray eyes lit up so brightly.

"I think he may be a genius," she said. "I'm sure he will grow into something great."

Anne put on the kettle for tea. "And how is your time at White Sands?" she asked.

"I enjoy teaching," Gilbert said. "The truth is, I find that I'm learning more now than when I was a student. I realize more and more how much I want to help people."

"Teaching is a great way to do that," Anne said.

"I want to do more," Gilbert said. "I want to fight disease, pain, and ignorance. I want to go back to college and become a doctor."

"A doctor?" Anne exclaimed. "How wonderful!"

"Do you really think so?" Gilbert asked. He was so glad that Anne was happy about the news.

"Your opinion does mean a lot to me, you know."

Anne blushed slightly and turned her head away. "You will make a great doctor," she said. Then, turning back to Gilbert with a smile, she added, "I can't imagine anyone better for the job."

Anne and Gilbert continued to talk about their plans for the future. What they hoped to do in ten years . . . all the things they wanted to accomplish. They were so lost in conversation that they didn't notice the time.

"Oh, my goodness," Anne suddenly exclaimed. "It's almost dinnertime. Marilla will be home soon. She was visiting her sick cousin again. I'm sure she will be exhausted from her trip."

"I should be getting home, too," Gilbert said. "My mother will not be pleased if I'm late for dinner."

Gilbert was only gone a few minutes when Marilla walked in the kitchen. Anne was still scrambling to make dinner.

"Oh, Marilla," she said. "You're early. I'll have food on the table shortly. Do you want me to make you some tea?"

Marilla sat down with a deep sigh. "Don't worry about me, Anne," she said. "I'm really not very hungry."

Anne noticed how tired Marilla looked. "Is everything all right?" she asked.

"I'm afraid not. My cousin Mary has died," Marilla said.

Anne gasped. "That is such awful news," she said. "What will happen with her twins?"

"They're with their minister right now, but they can't stay for long."

"And Mary's brother?" Anne asked. "Has anyone heard from him?"

"He is getting married in the New Year and can't take the twins before then," Marilla said.

"It would be so sad if they were sent to an orphanage until then," Anne said. "Even after all these years, I still remember life in an orphanage. I always felt so lonely."

Marilla sat quietly for a few minutes, then looked at Anne. Without saying a word, Anne understood.

"You're going to bring the twins here, aren't you?" Anne asked.

"Just until their uncle can take them next spring," she said.

"Marilla," Anne exclaimed. "I think that is a perfectly wonderful and splendid idea."

CHAPTER 6

Marilla Arrives with Twins

Mrs. Rachel Lynde was sitting at her window working on a quilt. Several years ago, sitting at the same window, she had seen Matthew ride past in a suit. He had been going to the train station to pick up Anne.

This time, she watched as Marilla rode past in the carriage. She was heading back to Green Gables.

"Marilla is returning from her cousin's funeral," Mrs. Lynde said to her husband, Thomas. He was lying on the living room couch. Mr. Lynde spent a great deal of time on the couch these days. He had been feeling unwell for quite some time.

Mrs. Lynde strained to look at the carriage as it passed. "And it looks like she has the twins with her," she said.

"Is that so?" Mr. Lynde said without opening his eyes.

"It seems that Marilla will have her hands full this winter," Mrs. Lynde said, shaking her head. "She is doing the right thing, though. And she does have Anne to help her. Anne is very excited about the twins coming to stay. That girl does have a way with children."

"Is that so?" Mr. Lynde said again. His voice was very soft.

When Marilla arrived at Green Gables, she was exhausted. The funeral had been hard, but the ride home had been even harder.

The twins—Davy and Dora—were as different as night and day. Dora was gentle and quiet.

Davy was wild and full of energy. He just could not keep still. Or stop talking.

He bounded out of the carriage and ran up to Anne. "Hello," he shouted. "My name is Davy. I've come to live here!"

"I know," Anne said, smiling. "I'm very happy about it, too."

"Davy," Marilla said. "If you can't be quiet, I'm going to send you to your room without dinner. It's been a long day, and I'm getting a headache."

"Oh," Davy said. "You wouldn't really send me to bed, would you?"

Anne laughed. "Davy, you'll soon learn that Marilla means every word she says. She's not one for idle talk."

Marilla sighed and helped Dora down from the carriage.

Anne walked over to the little girl. "Hello there," she said. "It's nice to meet you, Dora. My name is Anne."

"Hello, Anne," Dora said quietly.

Anne knelt down before her. "I'm glad you can stay with us for a while. Would you like to come in for some dinner?"

"Yes, Anne," she said rather seriously. "That would be nice."

All through dinner, Dora behaved like a perfect lady. Davy, however, caused nonstop trouble. When Marilla tried to correct him, he said he had no choice.

"I'm too hungry to be polite," he said. "Dora doesn't need to eat as much as me. She doesn't get as much exercise because she's so quiet. Also, it's been ages since we had cake—or real plums! Mother was too sick to make us one."

Anne could not help laughing. She cut him another big piece of cake before Marilla could object.

In his first week at Green Gables, Davy found time to get in numerous scrapes. He dropped a caterpillar down his sister's dress. He tried to keep a toad in his bed. He even convinced Dora to walk along the fence. She fell in the mud and ruined her dress, and then he locked her inside Mr. Harrison's woodshed. The poor girl was very upset when Anne opened the door to let her out.

Davy was not a mean boy. He simply did not think. He was good-natured and laughed often, but he always found trouble.

Davy adored Anne. He desperately wanted to impress her. He tried to not get into scrapes, but they just seemed to happen. He wished he could be more like Paul Irving. Davy had heard Anne speak about Paul, and she always said wonderful things. Davy was very jealous of the older boy.

"I suppose Paul Irving wouldn't knock the butter over during a meal," he sulked one night after he knocked the butter off the table.

"Paul is very careful," Anne said. "Although he is four years older than you. And accidents do happen."

Davy was not convinced. He knew that Anne was very fond of Paul. From that moment on, Davy considered Paul his greatest rival.

When he went to bed that night, Davy promised himself that he would be as polite and careful as Paul. Unfortunately, he had forgotten all about his promise by the next morning, getting into several scrapes even before noon.

CHAPTER 7

The Community Hall Disaster

ொ

The Avonlea Village Improvement Society did not get off to a good start. Their first project was to paint the Community Hall. The committee—after much discussion—chose the color green. "A very pretty green," as Anne put it.

Mr. Joshua Pye was hired to paint the hall. Mr. Roger Pye, one of his cousins, drove to Carmody to buy the paint. He delivered it to Joshua on a Thursday. By the time Mrs. Rachel Lynde rode past the hall on the Friday, Joshua was already done.

Mrs. Lynde did not stop to admire Joshua's

fine work, though. Instead, she rushed over to Green Gables.

"Marilla," Mrs. Lynde called. "You'll never believe it!"

"Goodness me," Marilla said and walked out the kitchen door. "What has you so excited?"

"That Joshua Pye has painted the hall blue," Mrs. Lynde said. "A bright blue!"

It wasn't long before the Village Improvement Society heard the news. They all gathered at Green Gables's front gate.

"It can't be true," Gilbert said. "We put so much thought into it. How did we end up with a blue hall instead of the green we picked?"

"It is dreadful, isn't it?" Anne moaned.

"It seems that Roger Pye bought the paint color number 157," Diana said, "when we asked for number 147."

"We should have gone to Carmody ourselves," Fred Wright said. "Joshua didn't know it was supposed to be green. Although, I must say, he doesn't seem too upset about it."

"We simply can't afford to paint it again. We'll have to live with the bright blue. But oh, the roof is so red! This is all the society's fault. Everyone will laugh at our mistake!" Anne sobbed while her friends tried to comfort her.

At first, the people of Avonlea did not think it was funny. They were furious that their donation money had been spent on such an awful color. Eventually, however, they realized how hard Anne and her friends had worked. It was an honest mistake that the hall was blue.

Some people even began to put an extra effort into helping the society with their projects. Major Spencer called to say that he would pull all the stumps from his yard, and Mrs. Spencer said she would help to plant flowers along the roadway. But Mr. Harrison offered the best advice of all.

"No need to worry, Anne," he said. "Everyone

knows that as paint fades, it gets uglier every year. But that hall is already the ugliest thing I've seen. It has to improve with age."

Mr. Harrison was right. People soon forgot all about the hall, and life in Avonlea returned to normal.

✑

Marilla, meanwhile, was kept very busy. Aside from the twins, her house, and her own troubling eyesight, she was called on more and more to help at the Lyndes'. Mr. Lynde was still not well, and it was hard for Rachel to get all of her work done *and* care for her husband.

So Marilla helped with the chores whenever she could. Rachel promised that she would not need Marilla for long. Marilla, however, suspected that Mr. Lynde's illness might be more serious than Rachel thought.

All of this meant more work for Anne, but she did not mind. She was happy with her work as a teacher and was no longer nervous around her students. She was happy to help out at home, too. She loved having the twins at Green Gables. Despite the accidents and new adventures, they made it a bright and active place.

It was not uncommon to see Anne walking with a spring in her step. In fact, she often talked to herself as she walked. She said hello to the trees. She complimented the leaves on their beautiful colors. When birds whistled, she whistled back.

One day, Diana caught Anne talking to herself. "Anne Shirley," she said with a laugh, "you only pretend at being a grown-up. You're still a little girl talking to yourself."

"Diana," Anne replied, "I was a little girl for so many years. I've only been a grown-up for a very little time. It takes some getting used to."

CHAPTER 8

A Golden Picnic

༄

Several months later, in the first days of spring, Anne and Diana met on the road.

"Diana," she said, "I was just on my way to see you. I wanted to invite you to my birthday party."

"Your birthday party?" Diana said. She was surprised. "Anne, your birthday was in March."

"Well," said Anne with a smile, "that is hardly my fault. If my parents had asked me, I would have told them I prefer a spring birthday. I do love the thought of arriving with the blossoms."

Anne already had her entire party planned.

"Jane will be in town, and I've also invited Priscilla Grant," she said. Priscilla was a friend from school. She was teaching in a nearby town. "I want to go into the woods. We can explore all those places we've never seen. Even as children we didn't explore all of the woods."

Diana did not seem convinced. "That sounds a bit . . . wet," she said.

"You should definitely wear boots," Anne replied, too excited to notice that Diana seemed unhappy about the plans.

⌒

The next afternoon, the four girls set off for their day in nature. Anne led the way happily. Flowers were blooming, and green leaves were sprouting on the trees. The colors of spring were so brilliant after the cold, harsh winter. It was a relief to step outside again and see the greens, reds, and blues.

Priscilla pointed out a patch of violets. "I do believe," she said, "that if a kiss could be seen, it would look like a violet."

"Oh, Priscilla," Anne exclaimed. She clasped her hands against her chest. "I am so glad that you said that out loud rather than keeping it to yourself. I think it's so sad when people keep beautiful thoughts to themselves."

"Look at this," Diana interrupted. "I've never seen this path before."

Anne followed Diana's gaze. "It's very over-grown," she said. "You have to look closely, but it is definitely a path."

"Should we follow it?" Jane asked.

"I don't know," Diana said quietly. "It might be dangerous."

"That's silly," Anne scoffed. "We can't walk away from an adventure!"

Anne was already partway down the path before her friends could disagree.

A few minutes later, the girls found an archway of cherry trees. The branches were hanging low with white blossoms.

"Why, it looks like an entranceway," Anne exclaimed. "It's like a secret garden."

Anne was right. The girls suddenly found themselves in a beautiful garden. It looked like no one had been there in years. There were some weeds, and parts were overgrown, but clearly someone had loved it once.

"How wonderful," Priscilla said. "This place looks perfectly magical."

"Why would such a lovely garden be back here?" Jane asked.

"It must be Hester Gray's garden," Diana said. "I've heard my mother mention it, but I've never seen it before. Do you know the story, Anne?"

"No," Anne said. "But you must tell it to us

now. You simply can't keep it to yourself for another minute."

The girls all found a place to sit down while Diana started her story.

"It happened a good many years ago," Diana began. "All of this land once belonged to Mr. David Gray. His son Jordan went to Boston for work and met Hester. They moved back to Avonlea, and built a house and this garden.

"Hester was very delicate. She was often sick, and the doctor said she wouldn't live long. She loved this garden, though. She used to sit out here wrapped in a shawl every day.

"Then, one day, Jordan carried her into this garden. He gathered roses and covered her lap with them. She smiled at him, closed her eyes, and then . . ." Diana could not finish her sentence. She could not say that Hester had died.

The other three girls all wiped tears from their eyes.

"That is such a wonderful story," Anne said. "So romantic."

"Do you know what happened to Jordan?" Jane asked.

"Mother said that he went back to Boston, where he died a few years later. He was brought back and buried next to Hester."

"I can certainly see why she loved this place," Anne said. "It's almost perfect, and so peaceful."

"She also planted those cherry trees. Hester told my mother that she wanted something to live on after her," Diana said.

"I wonder if we can find anything else as peaceful in the woods," Anne said as the girls continued to explore. They found other paths to follow and many more nooks and crannies—but nothing as interesting as Hester's garden. Eventually, they sat down again beside a flowing brook.

Anne opened up her basket and offered sandwiches to her friends. It was a simple meal but delicious, especially after so much walking. They happily ate and talked about their adventures.

"Look over there," Anne said. "Do you see that poem?"

"See that poem?" Jane said. "Whatever are you talking about, Anne?"

"Just look down the brook. Do you see that beautiful moss-covered log?" Anne asked.

"I would call it a picture," Jane sniffed. "Poems are words on a page."

"Oh, no," Anne shook her head. "That is where poems end up. Poems start right there. They start with a beautiful view. They start with something inspiring."

"Oh, Anne," Diana laughed. "You really do have a unique way of looking at the world."

Anne did not respond. She was already lost in thought. She was staring into the distance and thinking about Hester Gray.

CHAPTER 9

The Beginning of Vacation

⁓

It was a Saturday afternoon in June, and Anne was returning from an Improvement Society meeting. Their little group had finally become quite successful. People voluntarily pulled stumps from their yards, fences were fixed, and trees were trimmed. The society members were all pleased. There was still one very important matter, though.

"Mr. Boulter still has that run-down shack in his yard," Fred Wright said. He shook his head in amazement.

"Maybe I should try talking to him again," Gilbert said.

"Oh, there's no need," Anne said. "We've tried and tried. I think we're just going to have to live with it."

It was hard for them to accept this after so much success. There seemed to be little choice, though.

Anne was deep in thought about Mr. Boulter's shack as she walked to the cemetery. She was taking flowers to lay on Matthew's grave. Suddenly she was startled back to reality by a little boy sitting on a stone wall outside the cemetery. It was Paul Irving. He was holding a bouquet of flowers, too.

"Good afternoon, Teacher," he called cheerfully.

"Paul?" Anne said. "What are you doing here?"

"I thought you might stop by today," he said. "You mentioned once that you like to come by

on Saturday afternoons. I wanted to leave some flowers on my grandfather's grave. I thought it would be nice if we went together."

Anne smiled. "Yes, Paul," she said. "I'd say that is a marvelous idea."

"The truth is, Miss Shirley," Paul continued, "I'd really like to leave flowers on my mother's grave, but her grave is very far away. So I thought I'd leave flowers in her memory instead."

"That's very kind of you," Anne said.

"It's actually her anniversary," Paul said. "It was three years ago today that my mother died." The boy sighed. "I still miss her so much."

"I'm sure you do," Anne said. She patted Paul on the back.

"It's hard to talk about sometimes," Paul said. "Grandmother is very kind, but she didn't know my mother well. And it's hard to talk to Father because he misses her so much, too."

"I'm sure it is very hard for him as well," Anne said, placing most of her flowers on Matthew's grave. She saved one to leave on Hester Gray's grave. Ever since that day in the woods, Anne had made an effort visit Mrs. Gray whenever she came to the cemetery.

"Father isn't an easy man to get to know," Paul continued. "But if you did know him, you would like him a great deal. He's very smart and kind."

"I look forward to meeting him one day," Anne said.

"Oh," Paul said. He looked away. "I'm not sure if Father will visit. He's a very busy man, you know."

"Yes," Anne said. "You've mentioned that before." Paul often talked to Anne about his parents. He was very proud of his father and missed his mother a great deal.

Anne and Paul walked together down the lane for a while. They talked about their summer plans and Paul's upcoming birthday.

"My father said he was sending me something very exciting," Paul said. "I think it might already have arrived. Grandmother was very secretive about a package that came yesterday. I think it must be my present."

Paul placed the flowers on his grandfather's grave. "I suppose I should be getting home," he said, "before Grandmother worries about me."

Anne said good-bye and continued home. She had only gone a short distance when she met Mrs. Allen, the minister's wife. She was on her way to visit Mrs. Lynde, and they decided to walk together.

"You must be looking forward to vacation," Mrs. Allen said.

"Yes," Anne replied. "Of course, I will miss all

of the children, but I am looking forward to the extra time."

"I saw Gilbert the other day," Mrs. Allen said. "He must be starting his vacation, too. Are you two still studying together?"

"Yes, we get together whenever we can," Anne said.

"Do you still have plans for college?" Mrs. Allen asked.

Anne grew serious for a moment. "I'm not sure," she said. "Marilla's eyes aren't getting worse, but they are not improving."

"There are also the twins to consider," Mrs. Allen added.

"Oh, I know." Anne sighed. "It feels wrong to say, but I do hope that their uncle doesn't send for them."

Mrs. Allen said good-bye to Anne when they reached the fork in the road. "I'll stop by to see you soon," she said. "I'll bring a pie for Davy. I'm sure he'll enjoy that."

Two days later, Marilla received the news. A letter arrived from the twins' uncle in British Columbia saying that he could not take them until the following spring.

Marilla and Anne were both pleased. Without looking, they each knew the other was smiling.

CHAPTER 10

A Chapter of Accidents

Anne woke up three times in the middle of the night. She was worried about the weather. The sky was clear—she could see stars—but she was worried that it might rain. She wanted everything to be perfect when Mrs. Morgan arrived.

Priscilla Grant was bringing her cousin to tea at Green Gables. Mrs. Morgan was a famous author. She had written several books—all of them romance novels with beautiful heroines—and Anne and Diana had read them all.

Diana arrived shortly after breakfast. She was carrying a basketful of food on one arm. On the other, she draped a white muslin dress.

Anne and Diana had planned their lunch down to the last detail. All of the heroines in Mrs. Morgan's books wore white muslin. Anne and Diana decided they should, too.

Anne sighed. "Oh, thank goodness you're here, Diana," she said. "I am so pleased. And now, we must get to work. I think we should decorate the parlor first. Priscilla said they would arrive at twelve, so we have plenty of time."

The girls got to work. They placed flowers all around the room. They even put a garland of flowers over the door frame. The parlor of Green Gables usually looked very clean but very drab. Now there was color everywhere.

Anne put her hands on her hips. "I think we should set the table," she said. "We should have a vase of roses as a centerpiece. Then each plate should have a rose as well. I think that will look very elegant."

"That's a wonderful idea," Diana said. "That's exactly what happened in Mrs. Morgan's book *The Rosebud Garden.*"

Anne smiled. She hoped that Mrs. Morgan would also notice the similarities.

Anne brought out a very special item. It was a blue platter from Josephine Barry, Diana's aunt. It was an elegant dish, much fancier than anything at Green Gables.

Anne had written to Miss Barry and asked to borrow the platter. She was very excited about this lunch and wanted to impress Mrs. Morgan. Miss Barry agreed to lend her the platter but warned Anne that it was precious.

"Now I am certain that our lunch will be perfect," Anne exclaimed.

By eleven thirty, everything was ready. The lemon pies were baked, and the chicken was cooked. They also had a lettuce salad, potatoes, beans, and peas.

The other guests—Mr. and Mrs. Allen, and Anne's old schoolteacher, Miss Stacy—arrived just before noon. Marilla, Davy, and Dora also joined the party. Now they only needed the guests of honor.

At half past twelve, Anne started to get nervous. She looked out the window repeatedly. She went to the front gate to watch down the lane. When she returned to the party, she was very upset.

"What if she doesn't arrive?" she asked.

"She must come," Diana said. "It would be too awful if she didn't."

While the adults discussed Mrs. Morgan's arrival, Davy kept himself busy. He slowly made his way from his chair onto the table and reached for the lemon pie. Unfortunately, he lost his balance. The chair slipped, and Davy and the pie went with it. They all crashed to the floor. Davy was fine, but the pie was ruined.

"Davy Keith!" Marilla scolded. "Didn't I tell you not to crawl on the table?"

"I don't remember," Davy said. "You've told me not to do so many things that it's hard to keep track."

Marilla sent Davy to his room without any lunch. He went up with his head hung low, and Anne promised to save him some chicken.

At half past one o'clock, Marilla finally spoke up. "Anne, you must accept the fact that they aren't coming," she said. "Everyone is hungry, and waiting isn't going to change that fact."

Reluctantly, Anne agreed. She and Diana went to the kitchen to bring out the food.

The dinner party was a success, but it was not an enthusiastic gathering. As they cleared away the food, Anne put Miss Barry's platter on a side table and went into the kitchen to make a pot of tea. She had just put the water on to boil when she heard a terrible crash.

She ran back into the parlor. There was Miss Barry's platter lying in pieces on the floor. Beside it was one of Davy's balls. She looked up the stairs and saw Davy standing at the top.

"Davy Keith!" Marilla exclaimed yet again. "Did you drop that ball on purpose?"

"No," Davy said. He sounded nervous. "I was just sitting here, ever so quiet, trying to listen to all of you. I dropped the ball by accident. I swear!"

Marilla sent him back to his room. "And this time I'll check on you, young man," she called after him.

Anne had to admit that the day was a complete disaster. She wondered how she would ever recover.

Late in the afternoon, Marilla brought a letter

to Anne as she sat in the kitchen. It was from Priscilla.

"Priscilla writes that Mrs. Morgan has a sprained ankle. She is returning to Toronto sooner than expected," Anne said. "I suppose it was too good to be true that Mrs. Morgan would be stopping here."

"Anne," Marilla said. "You shouldn't take these things so seriously."

"How will I replace Miss Barry's platter?" Anne sighed. "She said it cost twenty dollars."

"I suppose you will have to pay her back the money," Marilla said.

"I suppose I will," Anne said sadly.

Marilla looked out the kitchen window. "Look," she said. "Gilbert Blythe is walking up the lane. If he wants to take you rowing on the pond, you should take your raincoat. It looks like it might rain."

CHAPTER 11

An Adventure on the Tory Road

❧

That night, Anne and Davy had a serious talk about dreams. At least Davy had a serious talk. Anne was trying not to laugh.

"Anne," he asked, "where is sleep? I know that sleep is where I do the things I dream, but I don't know how I get there. Or how I get back."

"I think sleep is found over the mountains of the moon," Anne replied.

Davy did not smile. "That sounds like non-sense," he said.

Anne let herself smile. "Yes, it is a bit of nonsense. I suppose you might be too little to understand."

Now Davy became angry. "It's not my fault that I am too little. I'm trying to grow. I might grow faster if Marilla would let me eat more jam."

"All right, Davy," Anne said. "That's enough for tonight." Anne gave Davy a kiss on the forehead.

"Can't I have a story, Anne?" Davy pleaded. "Something with soldiers and fighting and interesting stuff like that."

Before Anne could reply, she was saved by the sound of Marilla's voice. "Anne," she called. "Diana is signaling for you. She seems quite anxious to talk to you."

Anne said good night to Davy and looked out the east gable window to see a light flashing frantically from the Barrys' house. It was their old code from childhood. It meant, *I need to talk to you right away.*

Anne wrapped herself in her white shawl and ran over to Diana's.

"I have good news for you, Anne," Diana said. "I've learned that the Copp sisters in Spenservale have the exact same platter as Aunt Josephine's. Mother is certain that they would sell it."

"Oh, Diana," Anne said. "That is wonderful news. I'll go over first thing tomorrow. You must come with me. I am too excited to go alone."

As soon as the breakfast dishes were put away and morning chores were done, Anne and Diana left for Spenservale. It was a very hot day, and the road was very dusty.

"I hope that it rains soon," Anne said. "The grass and fields are so dry. Mr. Harrison says his cows can hardly find any grass to eat. I think it's very hard for everyone."

The girls turned onto Tory Road. They were looking for a white house with a neat and perfect yard. Diana's mother had said the Copps' home was so tidy, it put Green Gables to shame.

"That must be it," Diana said, pointing to a house so white that it was almost blinding. They drove into the lane.

"Oh, no," Anne said. "It looks like no one is home. The shades are down."

They knocked on the front door, but no one answered.

"What should we do?" Anne asked. "Should we wait until they return? We don't know how long that may be. I'm going into town tomorrow to see your Aunt Josephine. I so wanted to have the platter to give her."

"There's a window without a shade," Diana said. "I'm sure it's the pantry window. You could climb on the shed roof and have a look inside. Do you think that would be all right?"

"I don't think we have another choice," Anne said. "We simply need to know if they own a platter. It would be different if we didn't have an honest purpose to our trip."

With Diana's help, Anne climbed onto the roof of a back shed. She leaned over to rest her hands on the windowsill. To Anne's great pleasure, she saw the blue platter on a shelf in the pantry. In her excitement, she gave a little hop— and promptly fell through the roof of the shed.

Anne dropped down to her armpits, arms spread wide across the roof, where she remained stuck. Her legs dangled below her into the shed.

Diana ran into the shed and grabbed Anne's legs. She tried to pull her down.

"No, Diana," Anne cried. "I'm stuck on splinters. It will never work that way. Can you find something for me to stand on?"

Diana found a barrel and dragged it over to Anne. It was just high enough that Anne could rest her feet. She was now standing on the barrel rather than dangling in the air.

Unfortunately, Anne still could not free herself. The splinters were too long. She couldn't pull herself onto the roof. She couldn't slip down into the shed.

"It won't work," Anne said to Diana. "Do you think you could find an ax? You could chop the wood around me."

Diana searched the shed but could not find an ax.

"Oh, dear me," Anne said. "It seems like it's my fate to always find trouble."

"Anne," Diana said, "you'll have to hold on while I go for help."

"No, Diana," Anne said sternly. "You cannot leave me here. I will be the laughingstock of the entire town if anyone hears of this. We must wait until the Copp sisters return and swear them to secrecy."

"But Anne," Diana said, "what if they don't return until after sunset? Or tomorrow?"

Anne sighed. "Well, I suppose," she said, "if they are not here by sunset, then you can go for help. We must be strong until then, though."

Diana knew there was no point in arguing with Anne. Her friend could be very stubborn.

Suddenly a low rumble was heard.

"Diana," Anne said. She sounded very worried. "I believe that sounds like thunder."

Diana ran to the other side of the house to have a look at the sky, and then ran back to report the bad news to her friend.

"There's a large black cloud heading this way," Diana said. "It looks like a terrible thunderstorm will be here soon."

"Oh, goodness," Anne said. "If only my troubles and mishaps could be more romantic. I wish I could be more like the heroines in Mrs. Morgan's stories. They would never be stuck in a thunderstorm while trapped in someone's roof."

Diana pulled the horse and buggy into the shed. Then she found a parasol and handed it to Anne.

Diana waited out the storm inside the shed with the horse, while Anne bravely held the parasol over her head. The rain was so heavy that Anne was quickly soaked.

When it was all over, Diana checked on her friend.

"Oh, please don't pity me," Anne said. "I've decided that this is quite the adventure after all. I plan to get home and write it all down so I don't forget a single thing. Besides, the rain was needed. The farmers and animals will be very pleased, and I will dry out soon enough."

Just then a carriage pulled into the lane. It was Miss Sarah Copp returning home.

Miss Copp was quite shocked by the scene she

found. She stared in amazement at the young woman stuck in the roof of her shed. It was quite the sight.

She was not angry, though. Diana quickly explained the situation and Miss Copp rushed to the rescue. She opened the back door of the house and retrieved the ax. With a few quick blows she freed Anne.

"Oh, Miss Copp," Anne exclaimed. "I must promise you that I only looked through your window to check for the platter. It really was very innocent."

"You both look very hungry," Miss Copp said. "Please come in for a bite to eat and we can discuss it all."

Miss Copp was right. The girls were starving and very happy for the offer of a meal. While they enjoyed the tea and sandwiches, Anne offered Miss Copp twenty dollars for the platter.

Miss Copp sat in silence for a moment and then agreed.

As the girls rode home in the carriage, Anne carefully held the platter on her lap. They were both laughing.

"I can't wait to tell your aunt Josephine about this," Anne said. "I think she'll enjoy the history of this platter."

"Be careful, Anne," Diana said. She smiled at her friend. "We're not home yet. Knowing you and the adventures you get into, anything could still happen."

Anne laughed. "Having adventures comes naturally to some people," she said. "You just have the gift for them or you haven't."

CHAPTER 12

Teatime with Paul Irving

～

Not every day was an adventure for Anne. There were many days at Green Gables that passed simply and quietly. These days, when nothing exciting or splendid happened, were the ones that Anne loved best. "It's a day of simple pleasures," she would say to Marilla. "When one event softly follows another."

It was on just such a day in late August that Anne walked to Paul Irving's home and found Paul lying under a tree reading a book of fairy tales. He jumped up as soon as he saw her.

"Oh, Teacher," he called. "I'm so glad to see you. You've arrived just in time for tea! You'll stop for tea, won't you?"

"Thank you very much," Anne said. "I would love to have tea with you. Will your grandmother be serving her delicious shortbread?"

Paul looked very serious. "I'm not sure that will happen," he said. "Grandmother doesn't like me to eat so many sweets. She might offer you some, though. I'll just promise not to eat any myself."

"That's very kind of you, Paul," Anne said. "I don't mind if your grandmother decides not to serve any shortbread. I came here to visit you, not to eat cookies."

Paul smiled. He took Anne's hand and led her into the house.

Paul's grandmother welcomed Anne. She put out the tea—including shortbread cookies— and they all sat down together. When they were done eating, Paul's grandmother went into the yard to hang up laundry.

"May I tell you something, Teacher?" Paul asked.

"Certainly," Anne said. "You may tell me anything you'd like."

"Mrs. Lynde visited us last week," Paul said. "She saw a picture of my mother and said she was pretty. Then she asked if I was ready for my father to get married again," Paul continued. "She asked if I was ready for a new mother!"

"Paul," Anne said, "that might happen, you know. People do get remarried."

"I know that, Teacher," Paul said. "I told Mrs. Lynde that Father did a fine job picking out a wife the first time and I was sure he'd do just as well when picking out the second. I only hope that he will ask my opinion when the time comes. That would be nice."

When they were finished their tea and cookies, Anne and Paul carried their dishes into the kitchen. They washed and dried dishes, then put them away.

Anne and Paul spent the rest of the afternoon talking and telling stories. They imagined what life would be like in a fairyland or if they lived on a star. It was a very pleasant day. They both had the same kind of imagination.

When Anne finally went home to Green Gables, she found a very different little boy waiting for her.

While she was tucking him in, Davy flopped onto his bed without a word. He was sulking.

"Davy," Anne asked, "whatever is the matter with you? Usually you want to tell me all about your day."

"What does it matter?" Davy sulked. "You're always going to like Paul Irving better."

"Davy!" Anne exclaimed. "I do not like Paul better. I like you just as much, but in a different way."

"I want you to like me in the same way," Davy said, his face buried in his pillow.

"We all like different people in different ways," Anne said. "You don't like Dora and I in the same way, do you?"

Davy thought about this for a moment. "No," he said. "I suppose not. But I like Dora because she is my sister. I like you because you are *you*."

"And I like Davy because he is Davy and Paul because he is Paul," Anne said.

Davy was convinced by this logic. He gave Anne a kiss good night and went straight to sleep.

Anne, meanwhile, decided to go for a walk. It was a beautiful moonlit night, so she walked over to the creek and sat down on the bank.

She was only there a few minutes when she

saw someone else walking toward her. It was Gilbert Blythe.

For the first time, Anne noticed that Gilbert was grown up. He no longer looked like a young boy. Anne also had to admit that Gilbert was handsome. He was not her ideal man, but he *was* handsome.

Many years ago, Diana and Anne decided on their ideal husbands. They must be tall, dark, and mysterious. They must have piercing and intense eyes. There was nothing mysterious about Gilbert. He was welcoming and kind.

Gilbert sat down beside Anne. If someone asked him to describe his ideal wife, he would describe Anne. In Gilbert's eyes, everything about Anne was perfect. Even those things that Anne disliked—her freckles and red hair— Gilbert thought were beautiful.

Gilbert never said a word of this to Anne, though. He was certain that she would turn him

away. Or laugh at him, and that would be ten times worse.

Anne and Gilbert sat by the brook for some time talking about the Avonlea Village Improvement

Society and the end of their vacation. Then he walked her home along the lane. They lingered at the gate as they said good night.

Marilla looked up from her sewing when Anne stepped into the kitchen.

"That must have been some walk," Marilla said.

"What do you mean?" Anne asked.

"You have the silliest smile on your face," Marilla said. She had always suspected that Anne secretly liked Gilbert as more than a friend, but she knew that Anne would never admit it.

"Oh," Anne replied. "Do I?" She looked at herself in the hall mirror.

"Well," she added, "you know how fond I am of summer walks."

Anne bounded up the stairs to write all the day's events in her journal.

CHAPTER 13

The Way It Often Happens

ᥫᑊ

The next afternoon, Anne was all alone at
Green Gables. Marilla and Dora were visiting
Mrs. Lynde and Davy was at Mr. Harrison's, so
Anne decided to make good use of her time
alone. She set to work cleaning and dusting the
whole house.

She put on a ragged old dress. It didn't matter
if the dress was soiled, because Anne planned to
wash the windows inside and out. She was also
changing the feathers in the comforters. All of
this was very messy work.

As she was racing though the parlor, she noticed her reflection in the mirror. The first things she saw were the freckles on her nose.

Oh, no, Anne thought. *I forgot to put my lotion on last night.*

A few weeks earlier, Anne had found a recipe for freckle lotion in a magazine. It promised to remove freckles if applied each night before bed. After a several weeks of using the lotion, Anne was certain her freckles were already fading.

"I'll just run to the pantry and put some on," Anne said out loud. "I don't want to slow the process."

Anne ran into the pantry and grabbed the lotion from the shelf. Using a little sponge, she applied it to her nose. Then she quickly ran back to her work. She was finished changing the feathers in her comforter in no time at all.

By now, Anne was covered in white dust and feathers. They were all through her hair. They covered her dress. They were even stuck on her face. Anne knew she was a mess, but she was pleased with her work.

Suddenly there was a knock on the door. "That must be Mr. Shearer, the butcher," Anne said. "Marilla said he might stop by."

Anne ran down to the door. She didn't bother to clean up because she knew Mr. Shearer wouldn't mind the mess.

Imagine Anne's surprise when she opened the door and found Priscilla Grant and Mrs. Morgan, the novelist!

"Oh, Anne," Priscilla exclaimed. She was shocked by Anne's appearance. "Did we come at a bad time?"

Anne knew that all of the heroines in Mrs. Morgan's stories could "rise to the occasion." She made a very quick decision that she would do the same.

Anne welcomed Priscilla and Mrs. Morgan to

her home. She offered to make some tea and served biscuits.

While Mrs. Morgan sat in the parlor, Priscilla helped Anne.

"I'm so sorry," Priscilla whispered. "I had no idea this was such an inconvenient time. My aunt surprised us with this visit, and I didn't have time to warn you."

Anne noticed that Priscilla kept stealing glances at her. She thought Priscilla was being rude—especially when she had arrived without warning.

When Anne walked back into the kitchen, she found Diana waiting for her. She grabbed her friend by the arm.

"Do you know who is in my parlor right now?" Anne asked excited. "Mrs. Charlotte Morgan! And here I am looking like such a mess. Also, I have nothing to serve her but cookies and tea."

Anne noticed that Diana was staring at her, too.

"Please stop it," Anne said. "You're making me uncomfortable staring like that. I know I'm covered in feathers. You don't have to make it worse."

"Anne," Diana said slowly. "It's not the feathers. It's your nose."

"My nose?" Anne said. "Has something gone wrong?"

Diana nodded slowly.

Anne ran to the hall mirror. She let out a small cry when she looked at herself. Her nose was bright red!

"Oh, Diana," Anne said. "How could this have happened? I put the lotion on as usual. It has never turned my nose red before."

Diana shrugged her shoulders. She was speechless. This was a strange adventure even for Anne.

Anne ran to the pantry shelf. A jar of red dye

sat beside her freckle lotion. She must have grabbed the wrong bottle.

Fortunately, the dye washed off easily. Anne went upstairs to change while Diana ran home.

The white muslin dress that Anne planned to wear was drying on the line, but she had a nice green dress to wear. Diana returned shortly wearing her own white muslin dress and carrying a platter.

"Mother sent this for tea," Diana said. It was a platter of chicken and bread.

The meal passed without any further problems. Everyone ate their food and enjoyed the company. Anne was surprised that Mrs. Morgan was older than expected. She was short and squat with gray hair. Anne had always pictured a tall, elegant woman. Mrs. Morgan was, however, a wonderful guest, and they had much to talk about.

After their visitors left, Anne and Diana recounted their day.

"I think it was much nicer than if we had expected them," Anne said. "We would have worried the whole time. And we would have spent all our time serving the meal. We wouldn't have had the time to sit and enjoy."

When Marilla came home that night, Anne told her all about the afternoon. Well, not every detail about it. She left out the part about her red nose.

Later that evening, Anne took the bottle of lotion from the shelf. She carefully threw away the lotion and washed out the bottle.

"Never again," Anne said. "I will never again pursue such vain things. It may work for people who are organized and disciplined, but it will never work for someone as prone to adventures as me."

CHAPTER 14

Sweet Miss Lavender Lewis

୰

One Friday night in September, Diana appeared at Anne's door.

"Anne," she said, "we've been invited to tea at Ella Kimball's home tomorrow. The trouble is, we can't use our horse and carriage."

"Marilla is going into Carmody with our carriage," Anne replied.

"So we have no horse." Diana sighed. "I guess we can't go."

"Why don't we walk?" Anne suggested. "If we walk through the back woods, we'll end up on

East Grafton Road. It's only about four miles. It shouldn't take us long."

The two girls decided this was the best idea. They agreed to leave the next day in the early afternoon.

⌒

Anne was enjoying their walk. She stopped to admire trees. She sniffed flowers. She recited poetry about nature and the sun. But Diana was getting nervous. She kept looking at her watch. "We need to hurry up," she said. "We haven't left ourselves much time."

Anne's dreaminess might explain her wrong turn. At the fork in the road, she led the two of them to the left. They should have gone right. When they exited the woods, they found themselves on a long grassy lane. Neither girl had seen this road before.

"This isn't East Grafton Road," Diana exclaimed. "Where on earth are we?"

"I think this is the Middle Grafton Road," Anne said. She was very embarrassed. "I'm sorry, Diana. I must have made a wrong turn."

"We'll never make it in time for tea now," Diana said. "Still, we should continue on."

"There's a lane with a gate," Anne said, pointing a little way down the road. "There must be a house at the end of it. We could go and ask directions."

The girls opened the gate. Tree branches leaned over the lane, creating a splendid roof of leaves. Neatly planted flowers lined each side of the path.

"What a romantic old lane," Diana said. "It is beautiful."

"It feels as if we are walking through an enchanted forest," Anne said. "I wonder if we'll find a sleeping princess at the end."

Just then, the girls turned a bend and saw the sweetest little house. It looked as enchanted as the lane.

"Oh," Diana said. "I know where we are! This is Echo Lodge. Miss Lavender Lewis lives here."

"Are you sure this isn't a dream, Diana?" Anne asked. "I'm certain that we've walked into a fairy tale."

Diana laughed. "Miss Lewis isn't an enchanted princess," she said. "She's an old woman who lives alone in this cottage. I've never seen her myself, mind you, but I have heard many stories. I think she is quite peculiar."

Anne walked through the garden at the front of the house. Every flower imaginable lined the yard. There was a bench to sit on and enjoy the garden and sunlight.

"I think the most interesting people are always peculiar," Anne said. "I'd like to believe that she is an enchanted princess. She's waiting in this garden until her prince comes and rescues her."

"Her prince already came," Diana said. "He came and then he left. It was a long time ago. My mother told me the whole story. Miss Lewis was engaged to Stephen Irving, Paul's father. Something happened—no one knows what—and Stephen left. He never came back to Avonlea, and Miss Lewis never married."

"Hush," Anne said quickly. "The door is opening."

A girl of approximately fourteen stepped out. She had a wide smile on her face and waved at Anne and Diana.

"Is Miss Lewis at home?" Anne asked.

"Yes, yes she is," the girl said. "Please come inside. Please, please, come in for tea."

Anne and Diana looked at each other and then stepped in.

The inside of the small house was as magical

as the outside. It was beautifully furnished. White muslin curtains covered the windows. Vases of flowers sat on tabletops and windowsills.

"She must be expecting company," Anne said. "The table is set for six."

"Good afternoon," a voice said.

Anne and Diana spun around to see Miss Lewis standing in the doorway. They expected to see a woman dressed like Marilla, with a plain dress and her hair pulled into a tight, very neat bun on the top of her head.

However, Miss Lewis had wavy gray hair piled gently atop her head. Her dress was flowing and colorful. She truly did look like a princess or queen.

"Carlotta the fourth said you wanted to see me," Miss Lewis said.

"Yes," Diana said. "I'm afraid we're lost. We're looking for the Kimball place. We've been invited to tea."

"Certainly," Miss Lewis said. "If you walk a little farther, you'll reach a fork in the road. Keep to the left; that's the East Grafton Road.

"You will never make it in time for tea, though," Miss Lewis added. "I would be very pleased if you would join us instead."

Anne quickly responded. "Yes, please. We'd love to! As long as we're not intruding. It looks like you're expecting guests."

Miss Lewis looked away, blushing slightly. "No," she said. "I'm afraid I'm just a silly old woman. I rarely have visitors, so I was pretending. I do get lonely. This house may be tiny, but it feels very large when you're by yourself."

"Then we are very glad to visit!" Anne said. "I'm always happy to meet someone with an imagination. I think it's a wonderful way to have a tea party."

"I am glad," Miss Lewis said. "I'll set the food out right away. Please have a seat."

In a few moments, Miss Lewis and Carlotta the fourth brought out sandwiches, cakes, and tea. They all sat down.

Miss Lewis asked them their names. "May I call you Anne and Diana rather than Miss Shirley and Miss Barry?" she asked.

Anne and Diana both said yes.

"I'd like to think that we've already known each other for years. I do enjoy the company of young women. I can pretend that I'm not so old when I'm with young women."

After lunch, everyone went into the garden. While Carlotta ran inside to get Miss Lewis a shawl, Anne asked a question. "Why do you call her Carlotta the fourth?"

"Her name isn't actually Carlotta." Miss Lewis giggled. "I'm just fond of the name. I've named every servant Carlotta, and she happens to be the fourth. It's silly, I know. It does amuse us, though."

It was Diana who broke the spell of the afternoon. "I'm afraid it's getting quite late," she said. "We should go to the Kimballs'. They will worry if we don't arrive."

Miss Lewis walked them down to the gate. "I do hope you'll come back and visit," she said.

Anne put her arm around Miss Lewis's shoulder. "Yes, I can promise that we will," she said. "We must tear ourselves away from this lovely afternoon. 'Tear ourselves away.' That's what Paul Irving says whenever we part. I find it such a romantic thing to say."

"Paul Irving?" Miss Lewis said. She sounded rather shocked. "I don't remember anyone named Paul Irving in Avonlea."

Anne was embarrassed. She had forgotten all about Miss Lewis's romance with Stephen Irving years ago. "He's one of my pupils," she said slowly. "He's from Boston. He was sent up here to live with his grandmother."

"Is he Stephen Irving's son?" Miss Lewis asked. Her face was quite pale.

"Yes," Anne said.

Miss Lewis took a deep breath, then smiled.

"It's been wonderful to meet you both," she said. "Please take some lavender with you. And please, come back to visit soon. I feel like we are already old and dear friends."

CHAPTER 15

Miss Lavender Lewis's Lost Love

〜

It was a cool morning in October when Marilla received a letter. It was from British Columbia, but it was not from Davy and Dora's uncle. It was from one of his friends.

"What does the letter say?" Anne asked. "It mustn't be good news. You look so serious."

"I'm afraid the news isn't good," Marilla said. She laid the letter down on the table. "Apparently, their uncle has died of scarlet fever. Now there is no one to take the twins."

"Does that mean they can stay here?" Anne

said. "Please say yes, Marilla. They belong here at Green Gables. This is their home now."

"Of course they'll stay here," Marilla said. "Do you think I'd turn them out?"

Marilla stood up from the table and went back to making bread. Even though she was trying to appear stern, Anne noticed that Marilla was smiling to herself.

The twins were also pleased to hear that they were staying at Green Gables. They, too, considered it their home.

⌒

It was proving to be a lovely autumn. Anne continued with her schoolwork and extra studies. She spent her free time with Diana, visiting with Paul, or stopping by Echo Lodge. Anne and Miss Lewis enjoyed spending time together.

It was on one of their afternoons together in

early December that Miss Lewis told her the story of her broken engagement. The sky was gray and the snow around Echo Lodge was piled high. Miss Lewis's mood was also gray. Anne noticed that her friend seemed a bit down.

"I guess I am feeling sad today," Miss Lewis said. "It's not something that you would understand. You are young and beautiful and full of life. It's a wonderful thing to be seventeen."

"But you are seventeen at heart," Anne said. She wanted to cheer her friend up.

Miss Lewis chuckled. "No, Anne. I am quite old. At least I feel quite old today. It seems like only yesterday that I was seventeen and had the world before me. Anything was possible.

"Now I am alone in this cottage and wonder where all the time went. Don't look so sad, Anne. Having you here cheers me up. I think we should make some candy and forget all about gray things."

Anne laughed. "Yes, that sounds like a wonderful idea."

So the two friends made candy all evening. They had a fine time. The tiny kitchen of Echo Lodge was filled with laughter.

When they were done, Anne and Miss Lewis sat down in the parlor. They lit the small stove and relaxed.

"Anne," Miss Lewis said. "Did anyone ever tell you about Stephen Irving and me?"

"Yes," Anne said. "I've heard some talk. I know that you were engaged once."

"It was twenty-five years ago," Miss Lewis said. "We were going to be married in the spring. I even had my wedding dress made. Stephen and I knew each other from a very young age. When I was six years old, Stephen told me he intended to marry me. I was so relieved that I wouldn't have to grow old alone."

"What happened?" Anne asked. She was so eager to hear the story that she was almost out of breath.

"We had some silly fight," Miss Lewis said with a sigh. "I'm sure you won't believe me, but I don't even remember why we fought. It was such a trivial thing. I was young, though, and full of pride. I thought he would come back to me. I thought I could be rude and mean and he would forgive me."

"And he just left Avonlea?" said Anne. "Was that all it took?"

"No, he did try to patch things up, but I was still mad. I was still too proud." Miss Lewis stared into the fire. "He asked for forgiveness and I turned him down. That's when he left Avonlea. I should have written him. I should have asked him to come back. When I realized that it was too late, my heart broke into a thousand pieces."

"I'm so sorry, Miss Lewis," Anne said and put

her hand on her friend's knee. "That is a terrible story."

"I haven't mentioned Stephen Irving in years," she said. "It was only when you mentioned his son that I felt strong enough to talk about him."

"Paul is a delightful boy," Anne said. "You would adore him. He has a truly wonderful imagination."

"I would like to meet him someday," Miss Lewis said. "Would you bring him around?"

Anne's gray eyes shone. "Yes, of course," she said. "I will bring him as soon as I can."

It was not until a month later that Anne was able to bring Paul to Echo Lodge. As soon as Miss Lewis saw him, her face went pale.

"You do look just like your father," she said.

Paul shook her hand wholeheartedly. "Everyone says that I'm a chip off the old block," he said.

"And everyone is right," Miss Lewis said. "You know, I knew your father when he was your age."

"Really?" Paul said. "Do you have stories? I would love to hear about his childhood. Father doesn't always like to tell those stories. He often gets a bit sad when he talks about Avonlea."

"Why don't we go inside," Miss Lewis said. She took Paul's hand. "We can have some cake and get to know each other."

Anne followed them down the lane and into Echo Lodge. She was smiling. She knew Paul and Miss Lewis would be fast friends.

CHAPTER 16

The Big Storm

 ⌒〜

It was springtime once again, and Anne was as happy as can be. April brought warm weather, and May was the same. One day at the end of May, though, it was much warmer than usual. The air was thick. It was hard to breathe in the heat.

All of the children were enjoying recess outdoors when Anne noticed some very dark clouds coming toward them from the east. Then she heard a heavy rumble of thunder.

Since it was already late in the afternoon,

Anne dismissed her students. She told them to rush home so they would beat the rain.

Mr. Shearer, one of Anne's neighbors, was riding by in his wagon and offered to take some of the children home. "I think the rest of you should consider heading to the post office," he said. "It looks like this storm will be a doozy."

After Anne was sure all the children were safely away, she took Davy and Dora's hands and they ran back to Green Gables as quickly as they could. They made it just in time. They were running up the front steps when the sky became completely black.

From the safety of their parlor, they listened to the loud claps and rumbles of thunder. It shook the entire house. The room lit up every time lightning flashed. Branches were ripped off trees. All the windows on the east side of the house were smashed. Anne, Marilla, Davy, and Dora clung to one another on the parlor floor.

Then suddenly, forty-five minutes later, the storm stopped.

Anne and Marilla went outside to check on the damage. The yard was a mess. Trees were knocked down, their carriage was turned over, and their barn door was knocked off its hinges.

"It does look bad," Marilla said. "But the important thing is that everyone is all right. We can fix all of this. Although, I must say, it will take some time."

"Look," Anne said. "Is that Mr. Harrison walking up the lane?"

It was. "I wanted to check that everyone is all right," he called.

"We're all safe," Marilla said. "We've suffered some damage, though. We'll have to replace a lot of windows."

"How are things at your place, Mr. Harrison?" Anne asked.

"Not so good," he said. "The wind knocked

the chimney down. Then all the wind blew down
the chimney and through the house. It was so
strong that it knocked Ginger's cage over."

"Is Ginger all right?" said Anne.

"He'll be fine," he said. "Although, I must say,
he is pretty angry about it."

Over the next few days, there were more
reports of damage and destruction. Thankfully,

no one had been killed. Neighbors helped one another with repairs. Marilla baked several cakes and brought baskets of food and jam to the families who'd suffered the most damage.

The only benefit Anne could see was that the shack on Levi Boulter's land had been knocked down. She felt a bit guilty about this sense of relief. When she spoke with Gilbert about it later, she said, "Well, that is one victory for the Village Improvement Society."

CHAPTER 17

Around Another Bend

Spring rolled on and soon it was summer. It was
on a warm day in June when Mr. Thomas Lynde
died. As soon as Marilla heard, she rushed to be
with her friend. Anne took care of life at Green
Gables while Marilla took care of Mrs. Lynde.

After the funeral, Marilla sat in her kitchen.
She was deep in thought. Anne waited patiently.
She knew that Marilla would speak in her own
time.

"I suppose that Gilbert Blythe is going to

college this fall," Marilla finally said. "I suppose you would like to go to college, too."

Anne looked at Marilla, confused. "Yes," she said. "But how could we afford to send me? You still need help around the house and with the twins. Your eyesight is still poor."

"I've been talking to Rachel," Marilla said. "Money will be tight for her without Thomas."

"Won't her children help out?" Anne said.

"They all have their own families, and some live far away," Marilla said. "She'll have to sell the farm. Rachel and I thought it might be best if she moved here. She could pay me rent, which could pay for your college. Also, she could help around the house and with the twins."

Anne thought about this for a moment. She had always wanted to go to college. Now that it was suddenly before her, she could scarcely believe it.

"Really, Marilla?" she asked. "Would it really be possible?"

"I've thought it through many times," Marilla said. "We can do it. I've always felt guilty that you gave up college on my account."

"Marilla," Anne said. "I didn't mind staying home. Not really. I've been very happy teaching these past two years."

"I know that you'd never complain," Marilla said kindly. "But I've always felt you should be in college. I'm glad that you'll finally be able to go. Would you like to, Anne?"

"Marilla," Anne said slowly, "I feel—I feel as if—I feel as if someone has just handed me the moon!"

That night, Anne lay in her bed thinking. It was going to be hard leaving Avonlea. She was very fond of all her pupils. It would be especially hard saying good-bye to Paul Irving. They had grown so close over the last two years.

However, going to college was an opportunity that Anne could not pass up. She handed in her resignation the very next day.

Most people were sad to hear that Anne was leaving. Only Gilbert reacted with pure excitement. They would now be going to college together!

Diana was much less enthusiastic. "It's going to be very lonely here next winter," she sulked. "What will I do without you?"

"You still have the Improvement Society," Anne said. "You and Fred Wright could continue with that good work." She was trying to cheer her dear friend up.

"I'm certain the society will fall to pieces with you and Gilbert gone," Diana said.

"Don't be silly," Anne said. "It's too well established. You don't have to convince people to help out anymore. Everyone can see how important it is.

"Also, I wondered if you could do me a favor," Anne went on. "Would you mind visiting Matthew's grave? I leave flowers there every week."

"Of course," Diana said.

Anne leaned backed against a tree. "I feel like I'm heading off on the greatest adventure of all," she said.

"You'll meet so many clever people," Diana said sadly. "I'm sure you'll forget all about us."

"I do hope that I make many new friends," Anne said. "But new friends will never replace old ones, especially you, Diana. You were my first kindred spirit."

"Anne," Diana said. "I have a very serious question for you. Do you have any feelings for Gilbert?"

"I think of him very fondly as a friend," Anne said. "But I don't think of him as a boyfriend. I don't love him in that way."

Diana sighed. "Don't you wish to ever be married?"

"Perhaps," Anne said. She looked dreamily toward the moon. "Perhaps someday when I meet the right man."

"How will you know you've found the right man?" Diana asked.

"I'll simply know," Anne said. "I decided that a long time ago, and I'll know when I see him."

"Anne, ideals change," Diana said.

"Mine don't," Anne said matter-of-factly.

"But what if you never find your ideal?" Diana asked.

"Then I'll remain alone," Anne said. "That is hardly a terrible fate."

"Miss Lewis certainly is a good example," Diana replied.

"Oh, Diana," Anne exclaimed. She took hold of her dear friend's hand. "I want you to remember one important thing. No one will ever mean as much to me as you. You were my first real friend and welcomed me to Avonlea. Nothing could ever replace that."

The girls hugged tightly. They both knew there was no replacing a kindred spirit.

CHAPTER 18

The Prince Comes Back

ഇ

The last day of school finally arrived. The children—even some of the boys, although they all denied it—cried while saying good-bye. Anne felt sad that she was closing this chapter of her life. She loved teaching. It would be hard not seeing these bright faces every day.

For the first two weeks of July, Anne stayed at Echo Lodge. It was a wonderful vacation. Anne brought Miss Lewis into town a few times. She even convinced her friend to buy material and pattern for a new dress.

"I feel almost shameful," Miss Lewis said. "A new dress gives me such joy. Does that make me vain?"

"I would hardly think that could be possible," Anne laughed. "You are far too generous a woman to be called vain."

Midway through her visit to Echo Lodge, Anne went home to Green Gables. She wanted to make sure everything was well with Marilla and the twins. On her way back to Miss Lewis's, Anne stopped in to see Paul.

She had barely stepped into the yard when Paul flew out to greet her.

"Teacher!" he called. "You'll never believe it. My father has come for a visit. He arrived this morning. Can you believe it?"

He took Anne inside.

"Father," he said, "this is my teacher, Miss Shirley. I've told you all about her in my letters."

Stephen Irving stepped forward and shook Anne's hand. He was a handsome, distinguished-looking man. He had gray hair and a wide, friendly smile.

"It's a pleasure to meet you," he said. "Paul talked about little else in his letters. They were all about his beautiful teacher, Miss Shirley."

"It's wonderful to finally meet you, too," Anne said.

"It was a real surprise when Father arrived," Paul said. He sat down between his father and Anne. "No one expected him."

"And I was surprised by how big my boy is," Mr. Irving said. "He looks twice the size he was when I last saw him."

The three talked for a while until Paul was called away by his grandmother. She needed some help in the kitchen. Anne and Mr. Irving continued to talk, but Anne could tell he was thinking about something else. Finally, he spoke.

"In Paul's last letter," Mr. Irving said, "he mentioned visiting an old . . . an old friend of mine. Do you know Miss Lavender Lewis well?"

"Miss Lewis and I are very good friends," Anne said. "As a matter of fact, I'm staying at Echo Lodge right now."

"I wonder how much you know about Miss Lewis's and my . . . friendship," Mr. Irving said.

"Miss Lewis told me all about it," Anne said "We are close enough to tell each other secrets. It's not something she would have told everybody."

Mr. Irving nodded. "I wondered if I could ask a favor of you?"

"Of course," Anne replied.

"I would like to visit Miss Lewis," he said. "Do you think I could stop by tomorrow? Will you ask her if I may come?"

Anne promised that she would ask as soon as she returned to Echo Lodge.

It was a strange moment for Anne. She was not sure how to open the topic of conversation with Miss Lewis. Finally, she took a deep breath and let it out.

"Miss Lewis," she said. "I have something very important to tell you. Can you guess what it is?"

Miss Lewis stared at her friend. Suddenly her face became very pale. "Stephen Irving has come home, hasn't he?"

"How did you know that?" Anne said.

"It was the way you spoke," Miss Lewis said. "I just knew."

"He wants to come see you tomorrow," Anne said. She was so excited that she could barely contain herself.

"Well, of course," Miss Lewis said. She looked out a window to disguise her emotion. "He's only coming as an old friend. There's no reason why he shouldn't stop by."

Anne had a different opinion on the matter, but she kept her thoughts to herself.

The next day, Anne was sitting on the front porch when Stephen Irving arrived.

"This is one place where time stands still," he said. "Not a thing has changed in twenty-five years. It makes me feel young again."

"Yes," Anne said. "But the prince has returned. Things are bound to change now."

Mr. Irving looked slightly sad. "Sometimes the prince arrives too late."

Anne led Mr. Irving inside. She took him to Miss Lewis in the parlor and closed the door after him. She and Carlotta went out to sit in the garden while Miss Lewis and Mr. Irving talked on their own.

About an hour later, Anne noticed the front door opening. *Oh, no,* she thought. *This is too soon. If he leaves now, he'll never come back.*

Mr. Irving had no intention of leaving, though. Miss Lewis joined him on the front porch, and the two walked through the garden, arm in arm.

Anne was so excited that she grabbed Carlotta by the waist. The two young women danced in circles. "It's all so wonderful," Anne said. "I can promise you, Carlotta. There'll be a wedding at the stone cottage before fall!"

CHAPTER 19

Poetry and Prose

ᔕ

The next month was a whirlwind of excitement for Anne. She was preparing for college and packing all her things. But it was the wedding that took up most of her time. Miss Lewis was getting married, and Echo Lodge was the center of activity.

Everyone was excited. Paul ran to Green Gables as soon as his father told him.

"I knew Father would find the perfect mother for me," he said. "I already love Miss Lewis, and now she'll be my mother. Even Mrs. Lynde thinks that Father made a good choice."

Anne laughed. "Well, that's certainly something when Mrs. Lynde approves."

In fact, Anne could think of little other than the wedding.

"It's funny," she said to Marilla one night. "If Diana and I hadn't taken the wrong turn that day, we never would have found Echo Lodge. Then I never would have brought Paul to visit and Paul never would have mentioned Miss Lewis to his father."

"You're always looking for the romantic," Marilla scoffed. "The truth is, two young people fought. They were too sulky to reconcile. He moved away and eventually got married. By all accounts, he was perfectly happy, too. Then his wife died. After a decent amount of time, he returned home to look up an old friend. There's no romance in that."

"I suppose there isn't much romance in it when you describe it like that," Anne said. She looked disappointed. Like someone had thrown a bucket of cold water on her.

"Although," Anne added slowly, "I think it's like that when you think of the world as nothing special. But if you look at the world as poetry," she continued, "it's much more romantic."

Marilla was going to say something else but decided against it. Sometimes, she admitted, Anne's way of looking at things was nicer.

Instead, Marilla asked, "When will the wedding be?"

"They will be married on the last Wednesday in August," Anne said brightly. "The ceremony will be in the garden near the rosebushes. It's the exact spot where Mr. Irving proposed to her twenty-five years ago. Now, that is romantic! Even you must agree, Marilla. Only Diana, Gilbert, Carlotta, Paul, his grandmother, and I will be guests."

"And will they all live in Echo Lodge?" Marilla asked.

"No, they will return to Boston," Anne said. "Carlotta and Paul will join them in September. But they will come back to Echo Lodge every summer. I'm glad about that. I'd feel very sad if Echo Lodge was left to wither away."

Anne was so wrapped up in Miss Lewis's wedding that she did not notice another bit of romance happening nearby. She stumbled on it one evening when she went to visit Diana.

She found Diana and Fred Wright standing together by the garden gate. Fred was holding Diana's hand and speaking in low tones. Diana was smiling sweetly.

Before they noticed her standing there, Anne quickly turned and ran home. As she sat in her room, she thought about what she had seen.

"Diana and Fred are in love," she said to herself. "It all seems so hopelessly . . . grown up."

Anne realized that she was upset by this thought. "How can I tell Diana all my thoughts?" she said out loud. "She'll surely tell Fred."

Anne understood that her life was changing. It was not just about going away to college. Everything was going to be different. Her Avonlea would not be the same.

Diana came to see Anne the next night to tell her the news. She and Fred were engaged.

"I'm so happy, Anne," said Diana, "I feel like I might burst."

"What does it feel like to be engaged?" Anne asked.

"It would depend on who you are engaged to," Diana said. She already sounded wise. "It's perfectly lovely being engaged to Fred," Diana continued. "However, it might be awful being engaged to someone else."

"That doesn't offer a lot of hope for the rest of us," Anne said, laughing. "As there is only one Fred."

"Anne." Diana was blushing. "I didn't mean it like that. You must promise me that you'll be one of my bridesmaids. No matter where you are, you must promise to come back for the wedding."

Anne smiled and hugged her dearest friend. Her eyes were filled with tears. "I wouldn't have it any other way," she said.

With all this talk of weddings, Anne could not help thinking about her own. She thought about the home she hoped to one day have. Of course, she imagined her ideal husband. It was the same ideal husband that she had imagined since childhood.

Strangely, though, Gilbert Blythe was also

present in her dream. He was helping Anne plan the garden and decorate the room. No matter what Anne did, Gilbert kept popping up in her dream.

The end of August finally arrived. It was to be a very busy two weeks. First, Miss Lewis and Mr. Irving were getting married. Then Anne and Gilbert were leaving for college. Then Mrs. Lynde was moving into Green Gables. All the changes were happening quickly.

On the morning of the wedding, Anne rushed to her window as soon as she woke up. "Oh, no," she cried. "The sky is so gray. Surely it will rain and ruin the day."

Carlotta and Diana thought the same thing. But Miss Lewis would hear nothing of it. "Let it rain," she said brightly. "We have umbrellas. I've waited twenty-five years for this day. A little rain won't ruin it for me."

And so Mr. Irving and Miss Lewis were married in the garden under gray skies. Everyone in attendance smiled and cried tears of joy.

As soon as they were pronounced man and wife, the clouds parted. Sunshine shone down on the happy couple.

"That must be a happy omen," Anne said. Everyone agreed.

Shortly after the ceremony, Mr. and Mrs. Irving left for their wedding trip. Anne, Gilbert, and Diana threw rice as the couple rode off in their carriage. Paul rang a bell to send them off with music.

After the decorations were taken down and all the food cleared away, Anne walked with Gilbert to his carriage.

"What are you thinking, Anne?" Gilbert said. "You look very far away."

"I was just thinking about Miss Lewis . . . I mean, Mrs. Irving and Mr. Irving," she said. "It's such a beautiful story. Separated for all those years, and then coming back together."

"It is very sweet," Gilbert said. He looked down at Anne's upturned face. "But don't you think that it would have been better if they'd never been separated? If they had spent all those years together without that misunderstanding?"

For a moment, Anne's heart fluttered. She had to look away. It was the first time that she had faltered under Gilbert's gaze. Anne felt odd. She felt nervous and happy. She suddenly understood how heroines in romance novels felt.

Perhaps she had been wrong about romance. Maybe it did not appear as a white knight or hero from a story. Was it possible that romance arrived slowly in the form of an old friend?

Anne quickly shook off these thoughts. She did not look at Gilbert as she walked toward his carriage. Something had changed in her. She was growing up. She was ready for the adult world of college and leaving home.

Gilbert wisely said nothing. He knew the next four years of college would bring many new things. He also knew that the memory of Anne's blush that afternoon would carry him through the next four years. He would wait as long as necessary.

What Do *You* Think?
Questions for Discussion

⁓

Have you ever been around a toddler who keeps asking the question "Why?" all the time? Does your teacher call on you in class with questions from your homework? Do your parents ask you questions about your day at the dinner table? We are always surrounded by questions that need a specific response. But is it possible to have a question with no right answer?

The following questions are about the book

you just read. But this is not a quiz! They are designed to help you look at the people, places, and events in the story from different angles. These questions do not have specific answers. Instead, they might make you think of the story in a completely new way.

Think carefully about each question and enjoy discovering more about this classic story.

1. How does Anne choose to spend her warm summer day instead of reading a book of poetry? How would you like to pass such a day?

2. Anne imagines what her students will be in the future. Have you ever imagined what things will be like in the future? What do you see for yourself?

3. Dora and Davy are very different from each other. Dora is very proper and well-behaved, while Davy is always getting into trouble. Which of the two are you more like?

4. How does Anne react when she finds Dolly in the milking pen? What is the biggest mistake you've ever made?

5. How did Anne feel on her first day of school? Do you remember your first day of school? Were you nervous?

6. Gilbert values Anne's opinion, especially about important decisions. Who do you turn to when you need advice?

7. Anne calls Paul a kindred spirit. What do you think a kindred spirit is? Do you know anyone who is your kindred spirit?

8. Why does Miss Lewis call her servant Charlotta the Fourth? Do you have a nickname? Where did it come from?

9. Anne says that there are two ways of looking at the world: as nothing special or as poetry. How does Anne view the world? How do you look at it?

10. Why does Marilla invite Mrs. Lynde to come live with her? Do you think that she did the right thing? Have you ever helped a friend in need? What did you do to help them? Did they accept your help?

Afterword
By Arthur Pober, Ed.D.

❧

First impressions are important.

Whether we are meeting new people, going
to new places, or picking up a book unknown to
us, first impressions count for a lot. They can lead
to warm, lasting memories or can make us shy
away from any future encounters.

Can you recall your own first impressions and
earliest memories of reading the classics?

Do you remember wading through pages and
pages of text to prepare for an exam? Or were you
the child who hid under the blanket to read with

a flashlight, joining forces with Robin Hood to save Maid Marian? Do you remember only how long it took you to read a lengthy novel such as *Little Women*? Or did you become best friends with the March sisters?

Even for a gifted young reader, getting through long chapters with dense language can easily become overwhelming and can obscure the richness of the story and its characters. Reading an abridged, newly crafted version of a classic novel can be the gentle introduction a child needs to explore the characters and storyline without the frustration of difficult vocabulary and complex themes.

Reading an abridged version of a classic novel gives the young reader a sense of independence and the satisfaction of finishing a "grown-up" book. And when a child is engaged with and inspired by a classic story, the tone is set for further exploration of the story's themes, characters, history, and details. As a child's reading skills advance, the desire to tackle the original, unabridged version of the story will naturally emerge.

If made accessible to young readers, these stories can become invaluable tools for understanding themselves in the context of their families and social environments. This is why the Classic Starts series includes questions that stimulate discussion regarding the impact and social relevance of the characters and stories today. These questions can foster lively conversations between children and their parents or teachers. When we look at the issues, values, and standards of past times in terms of how we live now, we can appreciate literature's classic tales in a very personal and engaging way.

Share your love of reading the classics with a young child, and introduce an imaginary world real enough to last a lifetime.

Dr. Arthur Pober, Ed.D.

Dr. Arthur Pober has spent more than twenty years in the fields of early childhood and gifted education. He is the former principal of one of the world's oldest laboratory schools for gifted youngsters, Hunter College Elementary School, and former Director of Magnet Schools for the Gifted and Talented for more than 25,000 youngsters in New York City.

Dr. Pober is a recognized authority in the areas of media and child protection and is currently the U.S. representative to the European Institute for the Media and European Advertising Standards Alliance.

Explore these wonderful stories in our
Classic Starts™ library.